For my best friend, Louise
- J L

LITTLE TIGER PRESS LTD,
an imprint of the Little Tiger Group
1 The Coda Centre,
189 Munster Road, London SW6 6AW
www.littletiger.co.uk

First published in Great Britain 2017

A CIP catalogue record for this book is available
from the British Library

 • ISBN 978-1-84869-673-0

Printed in China • LTP/1400/1822/0217

1 3 5 7 9 10 8 6 4 2

The Only Lonely PANDA

Jonny Lambert

LITTLE TIGER
LONDON

Deep in the dewy forest,
where flamingos danced
and butterflies fluttered,
Panda sat alone.

"I wish I had a friend," he sighed.

Then Panda saw her.
"Wowee . . . Look! Maybe she
will be my friend."

But Panda didn't know
how to make friends.
"I wonder what the other animals do?"
he thought.

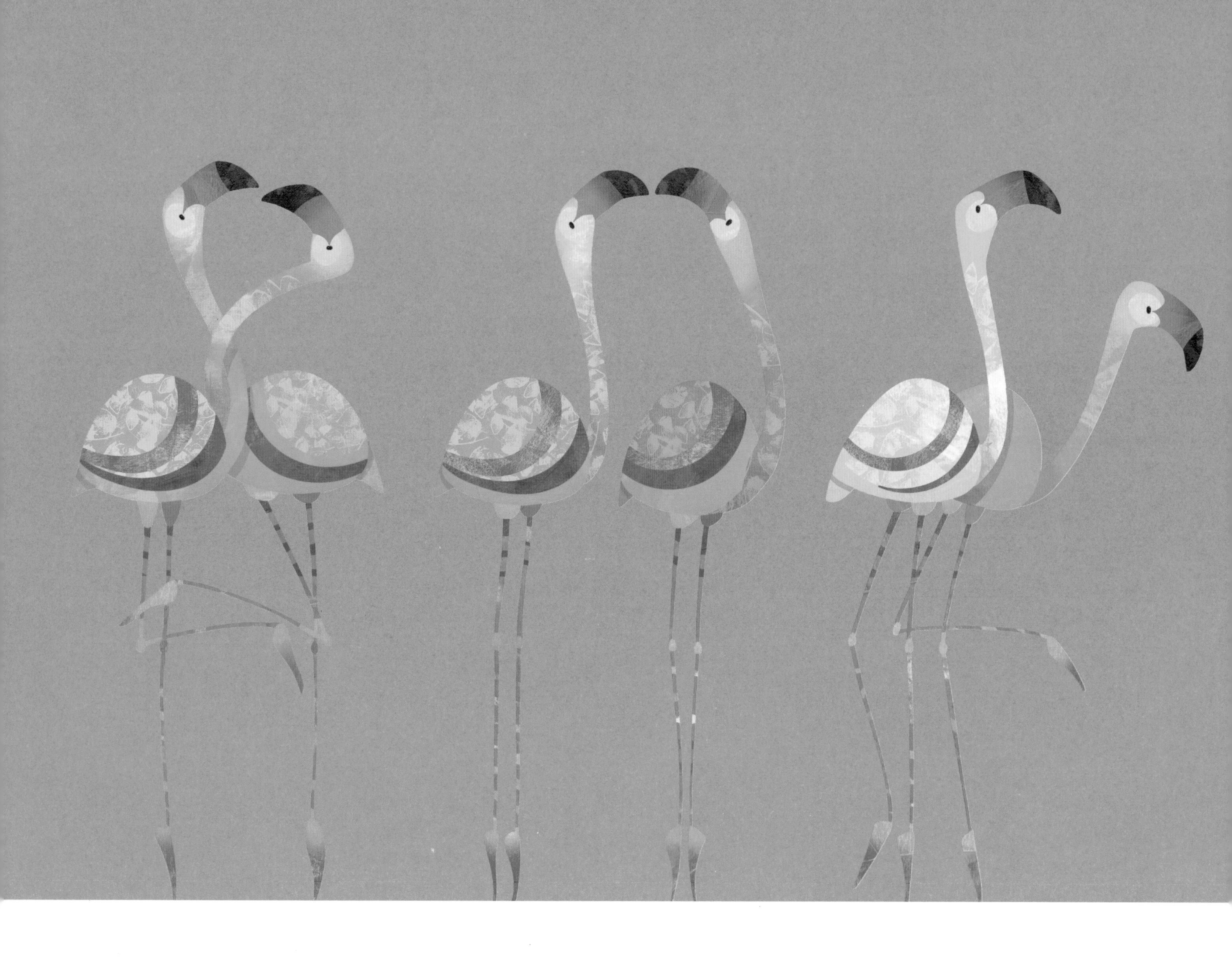

Graceful flamingos made friends by dancing together.

"That's it!" Panda exclaimed. "I will dance . . ."

"... like a fluffy flamingo.

Then the panda will be my friend.

How could anything

possibly

go . . .”

“. . . wrong.

Oof!”

Panda picked himself up and watched playful sifakas
make friends by bouncing and pogoing together.
"Brilliant!"
Panda cried.
"I will bounce instead . . ."

"... like a springy sifaka.

Then the panda will
definitely be my friend.

Whoopee!
Watch me fly!
Weehee!”

"Oomph!"

Down on the ground, Panda spotted two blue-footed boobies.

"Aha," he said. "I will **stomp** and **strut** like a booby, then we will be friends.

Now, where did she go?"
But Panda hadn't looked very far before . . .

. . . he spotted a **handsome peacock.**

"Feathers!" Panda whooped.

"If I had a dazzling tail, she'd surely be my friend.

All I need is one or two . . .

Yikes!

Sorry!"

"Phewee!" Panda puffed.
"Who needs fancy feathers anyway?"
Panda picked up some bamboo and
waggled his bottom.

“This tail waggle will surely succeed!

Here we go . . .”

“Poop.”

Panda sighed.
"She will *never ever* be my friend."
And he plodded off to get his dinner.

Deep in the dewy forest,
where sifakas bounced
and peacocks pranced,
Panda sat eating alone . . .

. . . but not for long.

"Oh, hello!" said the other panda.
"That looks tasty."

"It's scrummy!" nodded Panda,
and then he had his best idea yet.
"Would you like to share?"

And so they did.

Among the lush leaves,
two pandas ate and played together . . .
. . . and became the best of friends.